FARMYARD FRIENDS

Freckles
the Pig

by Lisa Mullarkey
illustrated by Paula Franco

Calico Kid

An Imprint of Magic Wagon
abdopublishing.com

To vegetarians everywhere: Freckles, Gaston, Golden Girl and Daisy thank you! —**LM**

To Nicoletta, thank you for your support, wisdom and friendship. —**PF**

abdopublishing.com

Published by Magic Wagon, a division of ABDO, PO Box 398166, Minneapolis, Minnesota 55439. Copyright © 2018 by Abdo Consulting Group, Inc. International copyrights reserved in all countries. No part of this book may be reproduced in any form without written permission from the publisher. Calico Kid™ is a trademark and logo of Magic Wagon.

Printed in the United States of America, North Mankato, Minnesota.
052017
092017

Written by Lisa Mullarkey
Illustrated by Paula Franco
Edited by Megan M. Gunderson
Designed by Christina Doffing

Publisher's Cataloging-in-Publication Data

Names: Mullarkey, Lisa, author. | Franco, Paula, illustrator.
Title: Freckles the pig / by Lisa Mullarkey ; illustrated by Paula Franco.
Description: Minneapolis, MN : Magic Wagon, 2018. | Series: Farmyard friends
Summary: Freckles the pig wants to help with fall cleanup, but he makes a muddy
    mess instead, until he finds just what his artistic side needs.
Identifiers: LCCN 2017930513 | ISBN 9781532140440 (lib. bdg.) |
    ISBN 9781624029912 (ebook) | ISBN 9781624029967 (Read-to-me ebook)
Subjects: LCSH: Pigs--Juvenile fiction. | Friendship--Juvenile fiction. | Painting--
    Juvenile fiction.
Classification: DDC [Fic]--dc23
LC record available at http://lccn.loc.gov/2017930513

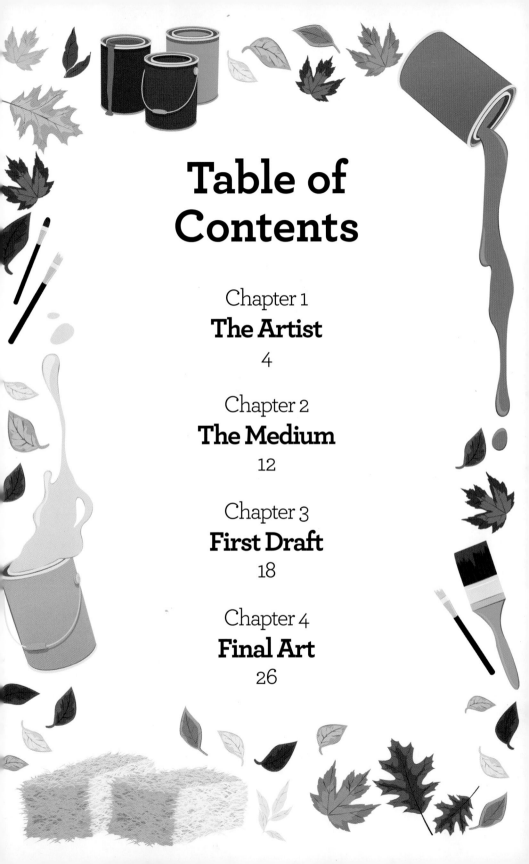

Table of Contents

Chapter 1
The Artist

Autumn arrived at Storm Cliff

Stables.

The leaves fluttered to the ground.

Flitter, flutter, flitter, flutter, flitter.

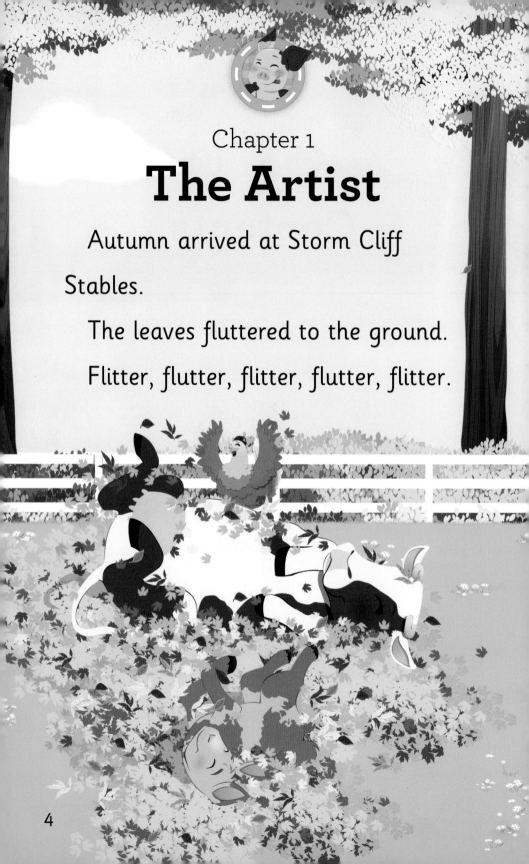

Yellow leaves fell.

Flit-flit-flit.

Orange leaves fell.

Flit-flit-flit.

Red leaves fell, too.

Flitter, flutter, flitter, flutter, flitter.

Daisy, Gaston, and Golden Girl watched Aunt Jane and the campers working. Then they spotted Freckles by his pen.

"Morning, Freckles," said Daisy. She swished her tail back and forth, back and forth, and back and forth again. "What are you doing?"

Freckles plopped in the mud. "I am splish-splashing in the mud!" He pointed to the sign. "I am a good friend. I am getting ready to work!"

Golden Girl squawked. "Work? It is fall cleanup. Not fall mess up! You are messy, messy, messy. You live in a pigpen. It is a pigsty!"

"BLEAT!" said Gaston. "Do not work. Come play with us!"

Freckles rolled in the mushy, gushy mud. "Not today! No play for me! Today I will work, work, work."

"Cluck," said Golden Girl. "Walk to the stables with us."

Freckles slid his hooves into the sloppy, gloppy mud. "Not today! Today will be different, my farmyard friends."

Freckles rolled in the squishy, squashy mud. "I will not play, play, play today. Instead, I will work, work, work. Just wait and see! I will be a good friend. A messy, messy, messy, hardworking friend!"

Chapter 2
The Medium

Gaston chewed and chomped on a can. "You are already a good friend."

Golden Girl flew up in the air. She landed on Daisy's head. "A messy one, but a good one!"

"I want to be a great friend to Aunt Jane, too," said Freckles. "She gives me slop each day. She scratches my belly and kisses my snout. She is a good friend to me. Today, I will be a good friend to her. I will help."

Freckles trotted over to the silo and tap-tap-tapped the sign. "I will spiffy up the barn."

His hoof left a muddy mark.

The friends laughed. Freckles snorted.

"You have all said the barn is dark and dank. It is gloomy and glum. Aunt Jane must think so, too."

Freckles held up his muddy hoof. "So today, I will change that by painting."

SPIFFY UP THE BARN

"Hogwash," said Gaston.

"That is plain silly," said Daisy.

"Pigs can't paint!" said Golden Girl.

Freckles snorted. "I will turn the barn into a masterpiece. Just you wait and see!"

Chapter 3
First Draft

Freckles trudged over to the mud puddle next to the barn. He closed his eyes. He pretended he was one of the most famous artists in the world, Pablo Pigasso.

Freckles dipped his hooves into the mushy, gushy mud. He dunked his snout into sloppy, gloppy mud. Then he ducked inside and began to paint.

With a swish, swish here and a swoosh, swoosh there, Freckles painted a picture next to Daisy's milking stall.

Freckles did a happy dance. "Just like Moooonet."

Freckles scooped up more squishy, squashy mud. With a splish and a splosh, he painted a picture of Golden Girl in front of her nesting box.

Freckles squealed. "Reminds me of Henoir."

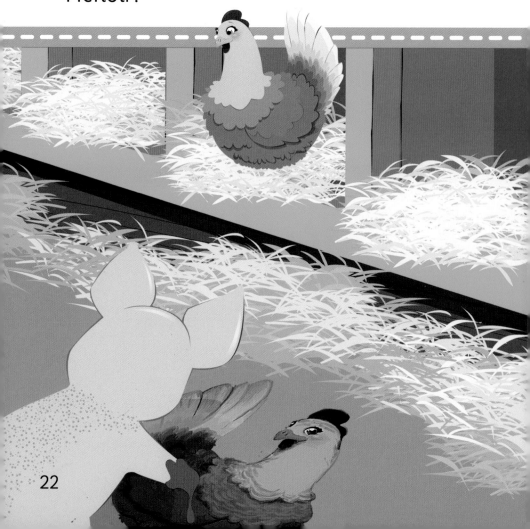

Then with a twirly-twirl-twirl and a curly-curl-curl, he made swirly skies and stunning stars near the haystack. Finally, he created a picture of Gaston.

"I am better than Van Gobble!" said Freckles. "Mud makes the perfect paint!"

Daisy frowned. "Your pictures look grimy and gritty. Everything looks mucky and a little bit . . ."

"Yucky," said Gaston. "The barn is still dark and dank."

Freckles gasped.

Golden Girl agreed. "A for effort! But the paintings do look a bit scribbly, scrabbly, smudgy, and . . ."

"Smeary," said Freckles. He hung his head low. "You all are right. Everything looks blurry. A bit bleary."

Then he remembered something he saw by the sign. Freckles perked up, up, up!

"Don't worry! Just you wait and see. I am going to turn blurry and bleary into something quite cheery!"

Chapter 4
Final Art

Freckles marched over to the sign. He spotted paper. He spotted paint cans.

There was red paint.

There was blue paint.

There was orange, green, and yellow paint, too!

"Yahoo!" said Freckles.

He looked to the left. He looked to the right. When he was sure no one was looking, he tip-tip-tipped the cans over.

Then he did another happy dance. He danced in the paint. He danced on the paper!

Tap-tap-tap. Swish-swish-swish.

One painting done!

Tap-tap-tap. Swish-swish-swish.

Another painting done!

Tap-tap-tap. Swish-swish-swish.

More paintings done!

Tap-tap-tap. Swish-swish-swish.

All paintings done!

When the friends saw the paintings, they went hog wild!

Golden Girl smiled. "Oh, my! I never knew I was this good looking!"

Daisy batted her eyelashes. "This one is udderly beautiful!"

"Bravo!" said Gaston. "These will change our dark and dreary barn to a bright and cheery barn!"

Later that day, Aunt Jane and Jaelyn walked by the paintings. Aunt Jane picked one up. "Super job as usual, Jaelyn. You are an amazing artist!"

Jaelyn shook her head. "I didn't paint these. I was with you all day."

Aunt Jane scratched her head. "So were all the other campers."

Aunt Jane looked around the farm. "Who could have painted these?"

Jaelyn saw Freckles sleeping just a few feet away. He was covered in paint. "You don't think . . ."

Aunt Jane laughed. "No! Everyone knows that pigs can't paint. Right?"